Fishes by Bria

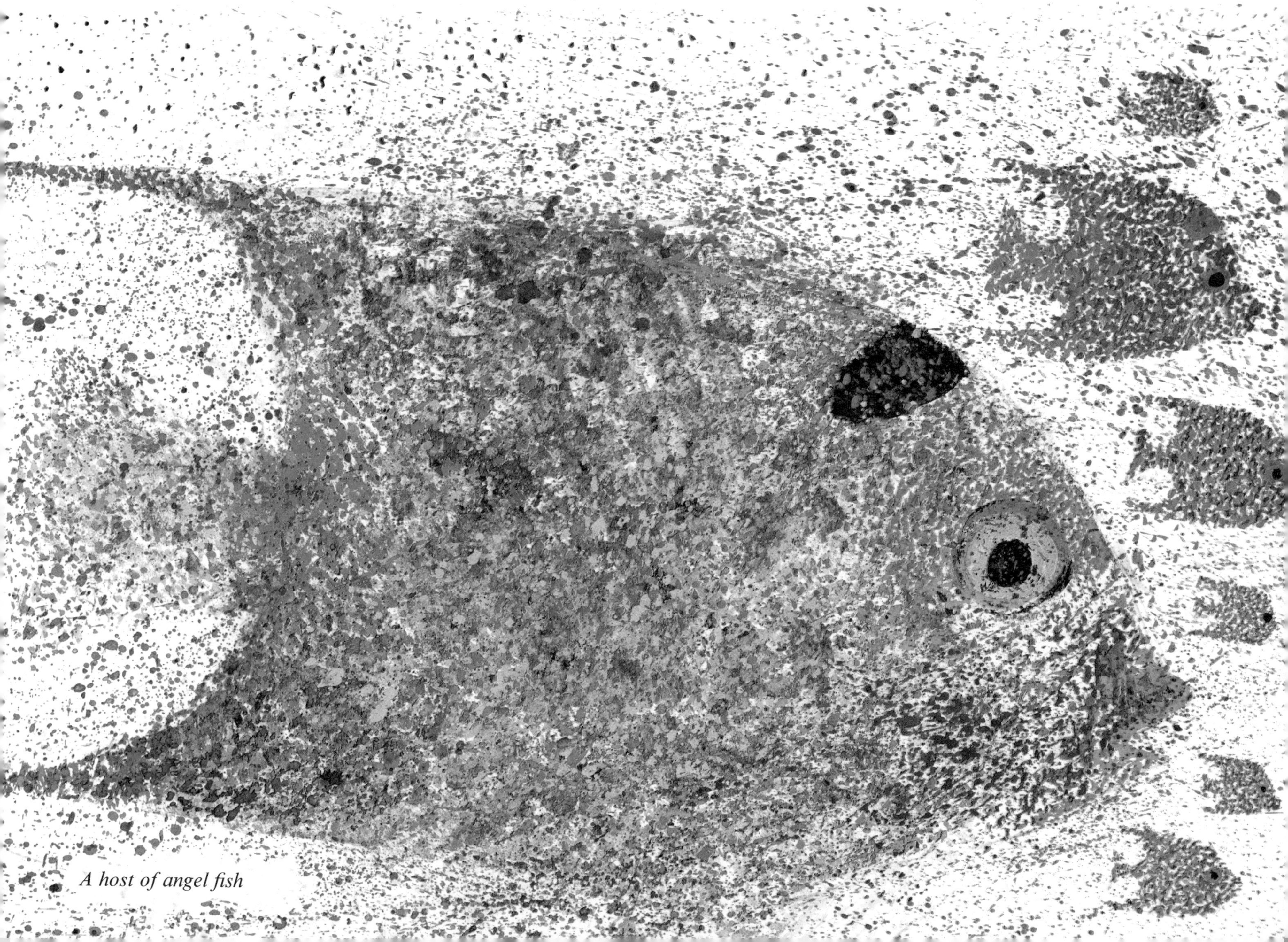

A host of angel fish

For Simon

A shoal of mackerel

Fishes by Brian Wildsmith

OXFORD UNIVERSITY PRESS

A cluster of porcupine fish

A school of butterfly fish

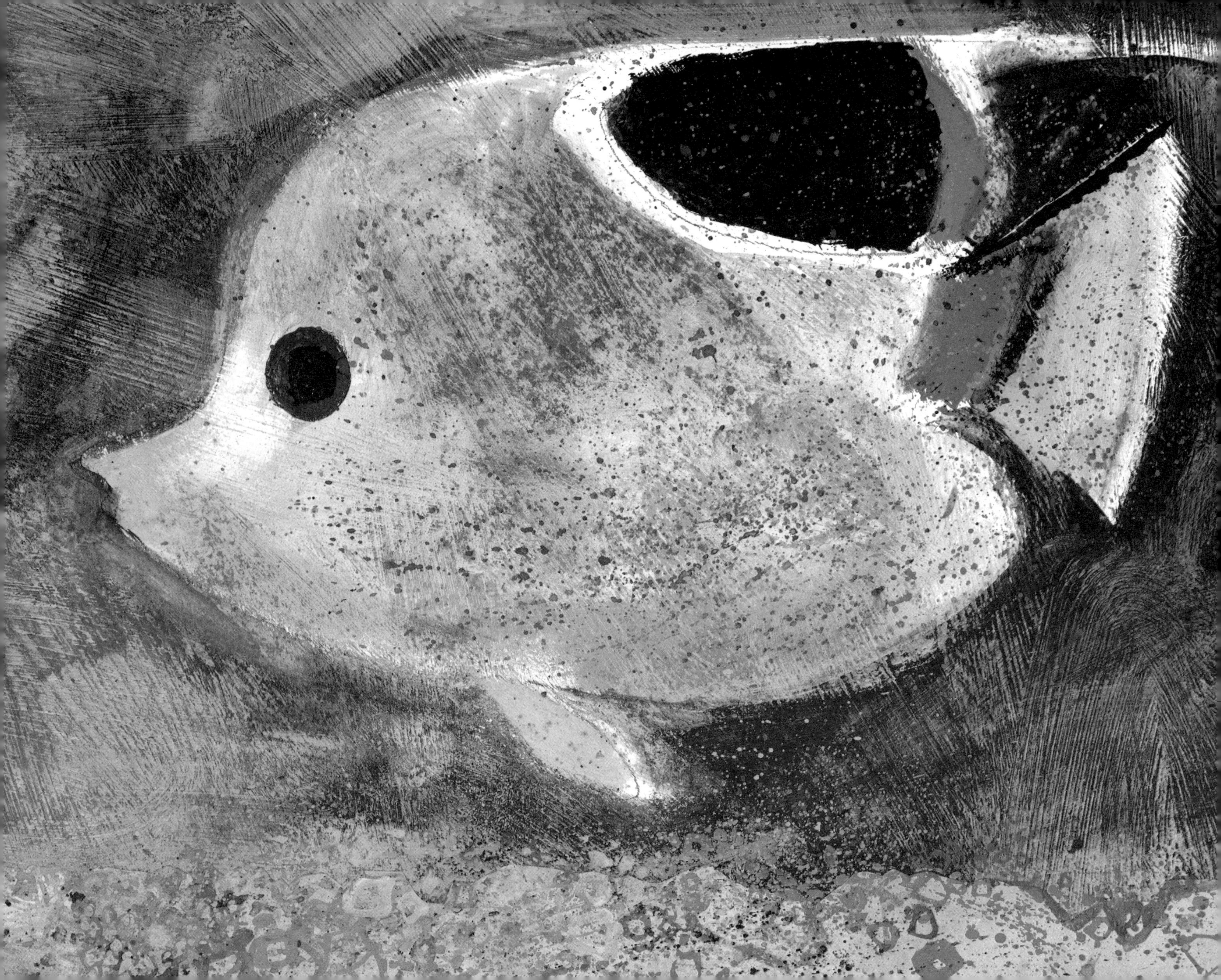

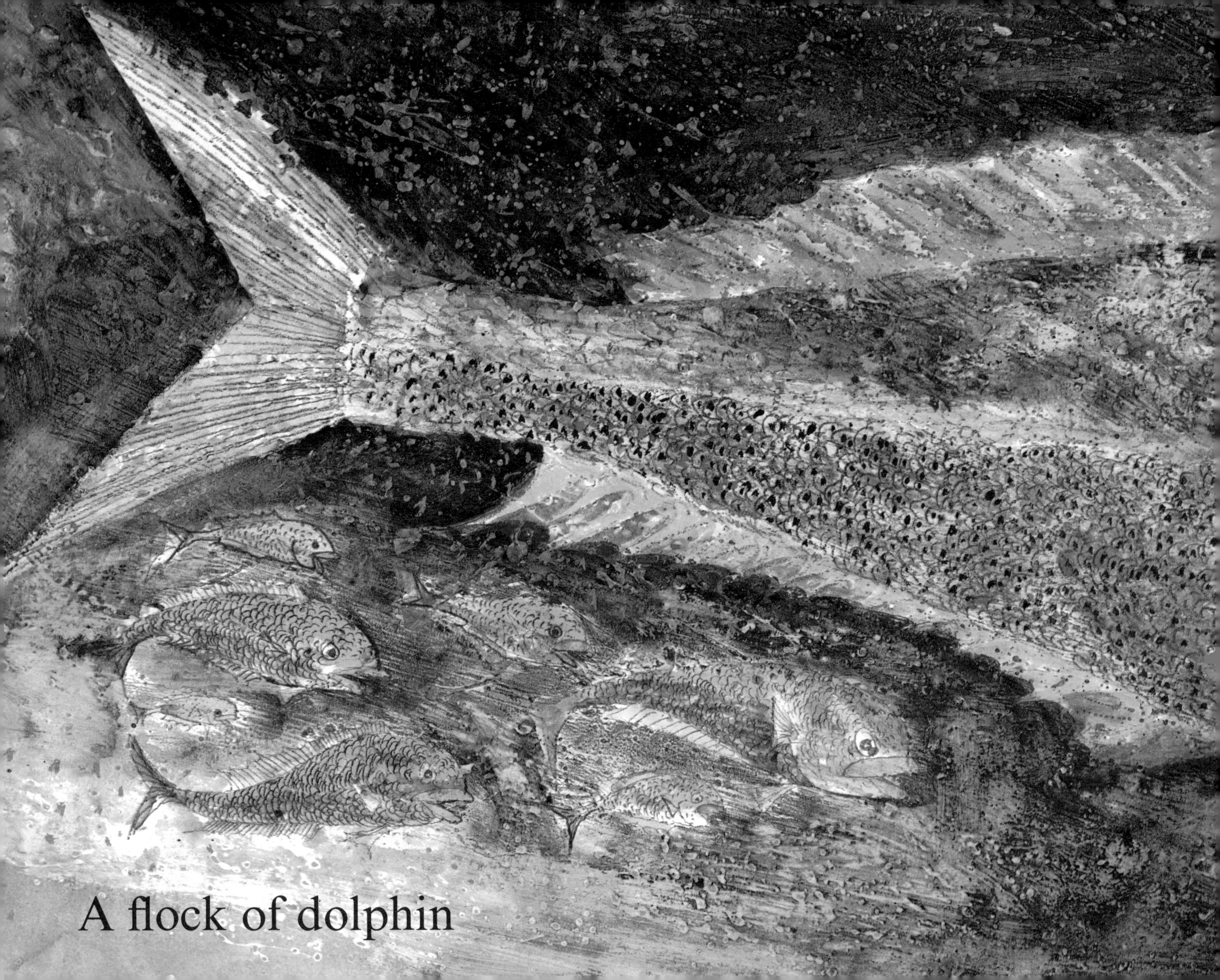

A flock of dolphin

A glide of flying fish

A company of archerfish

A hover of trout

A battery of barracuda

A herd
of sea horses

A party of rainbow fish

A fleet of bass

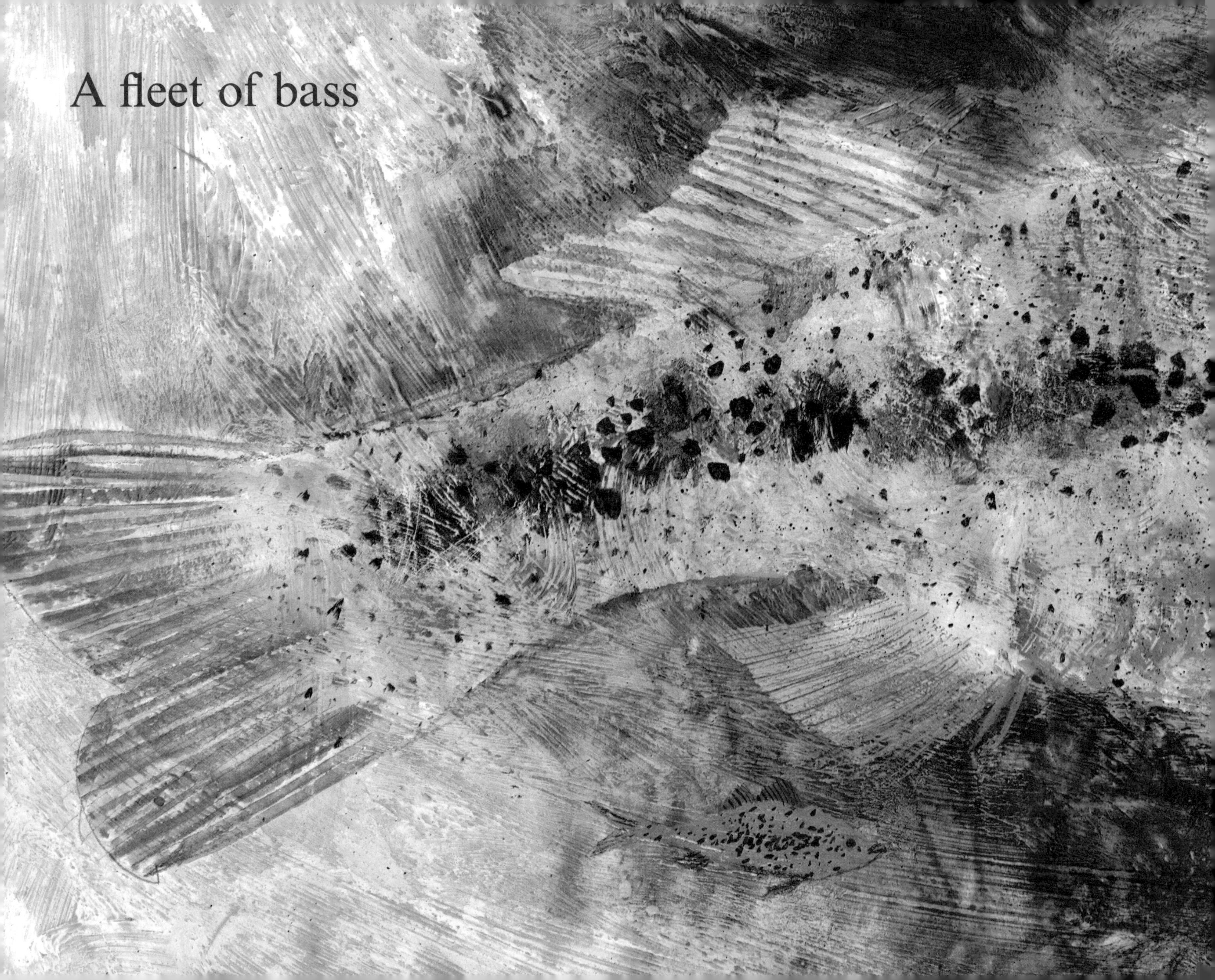

A swarm of dragonet fish

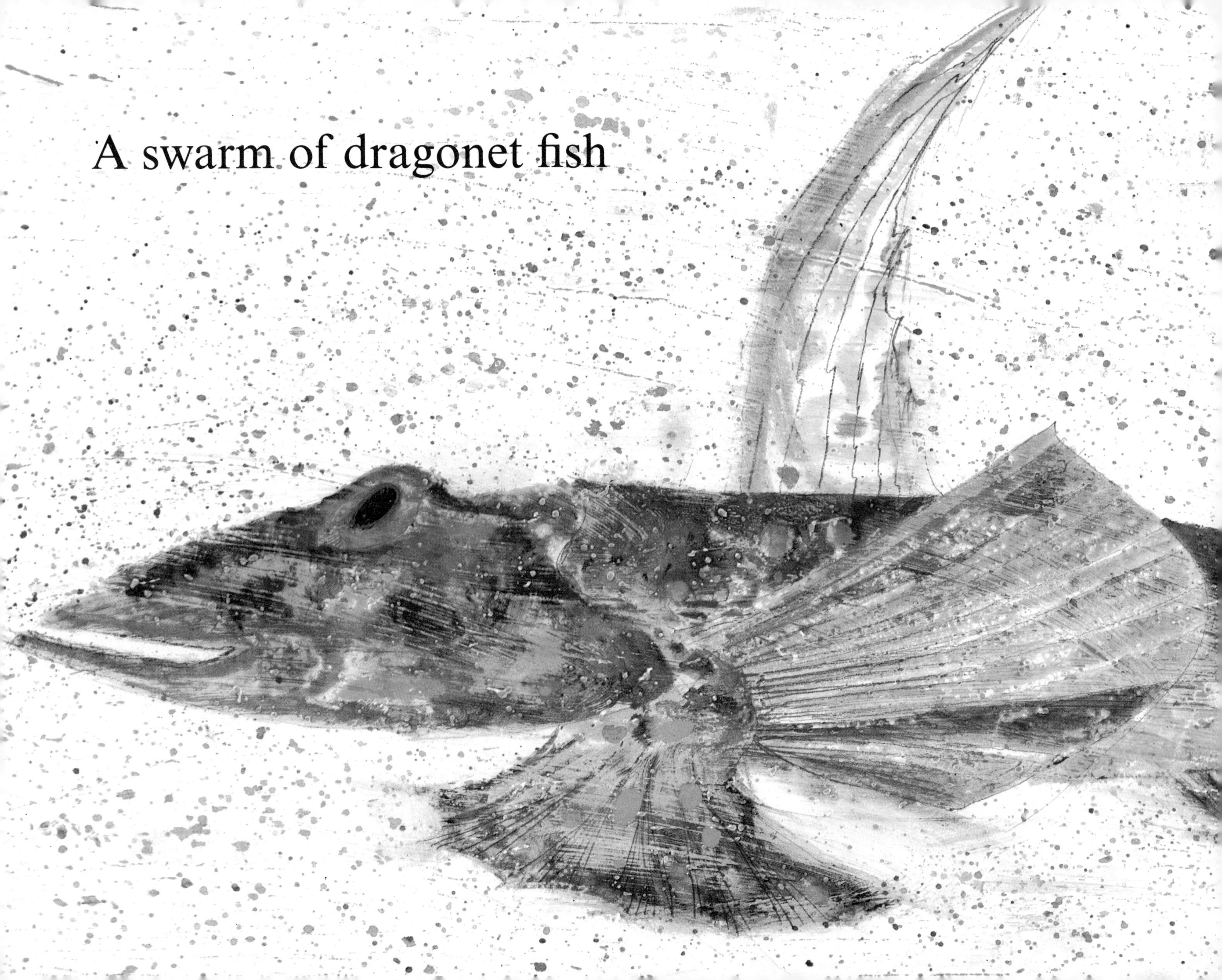

A flotilla of swordfish

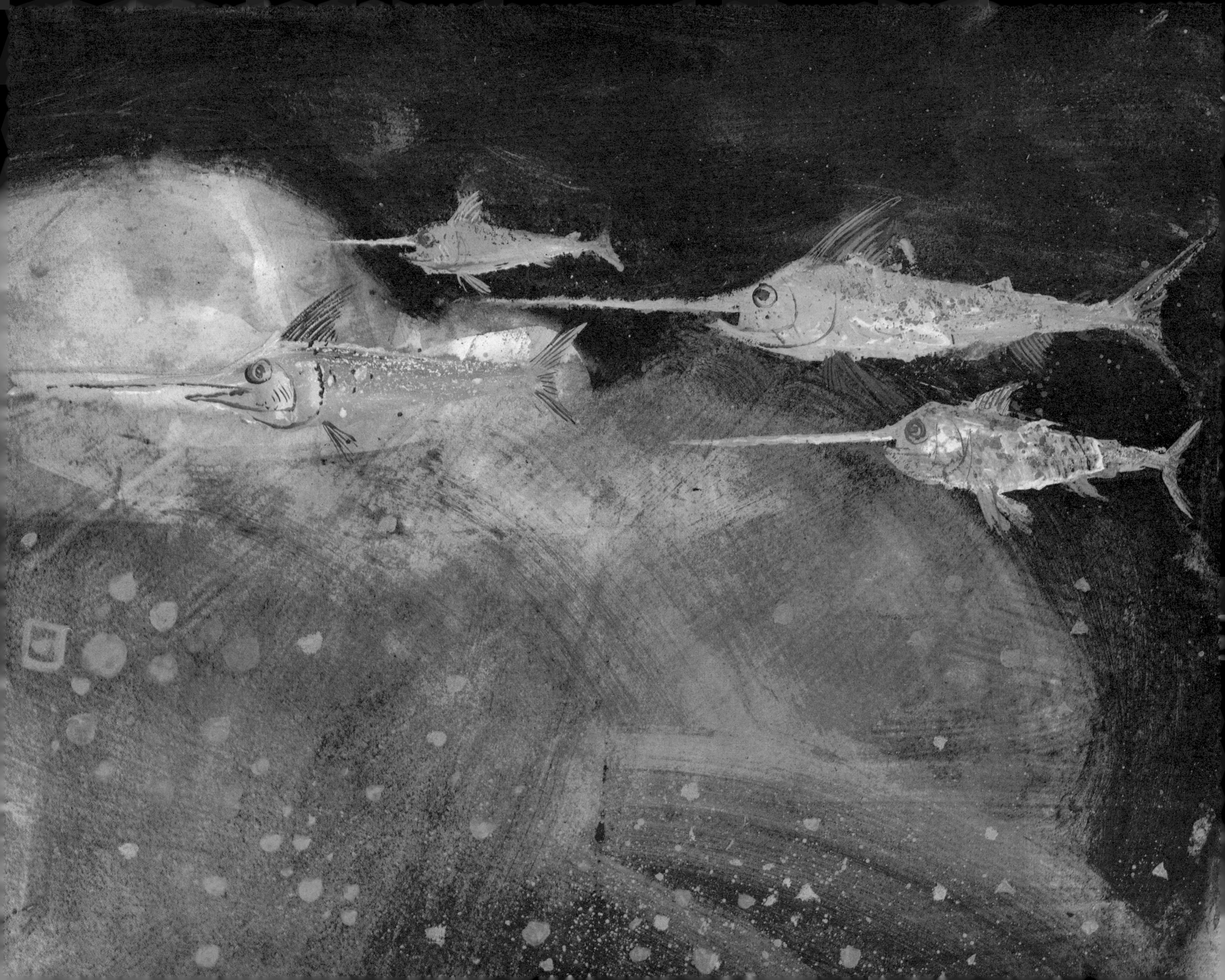

A spread of sticklebacks

A stream of minnows

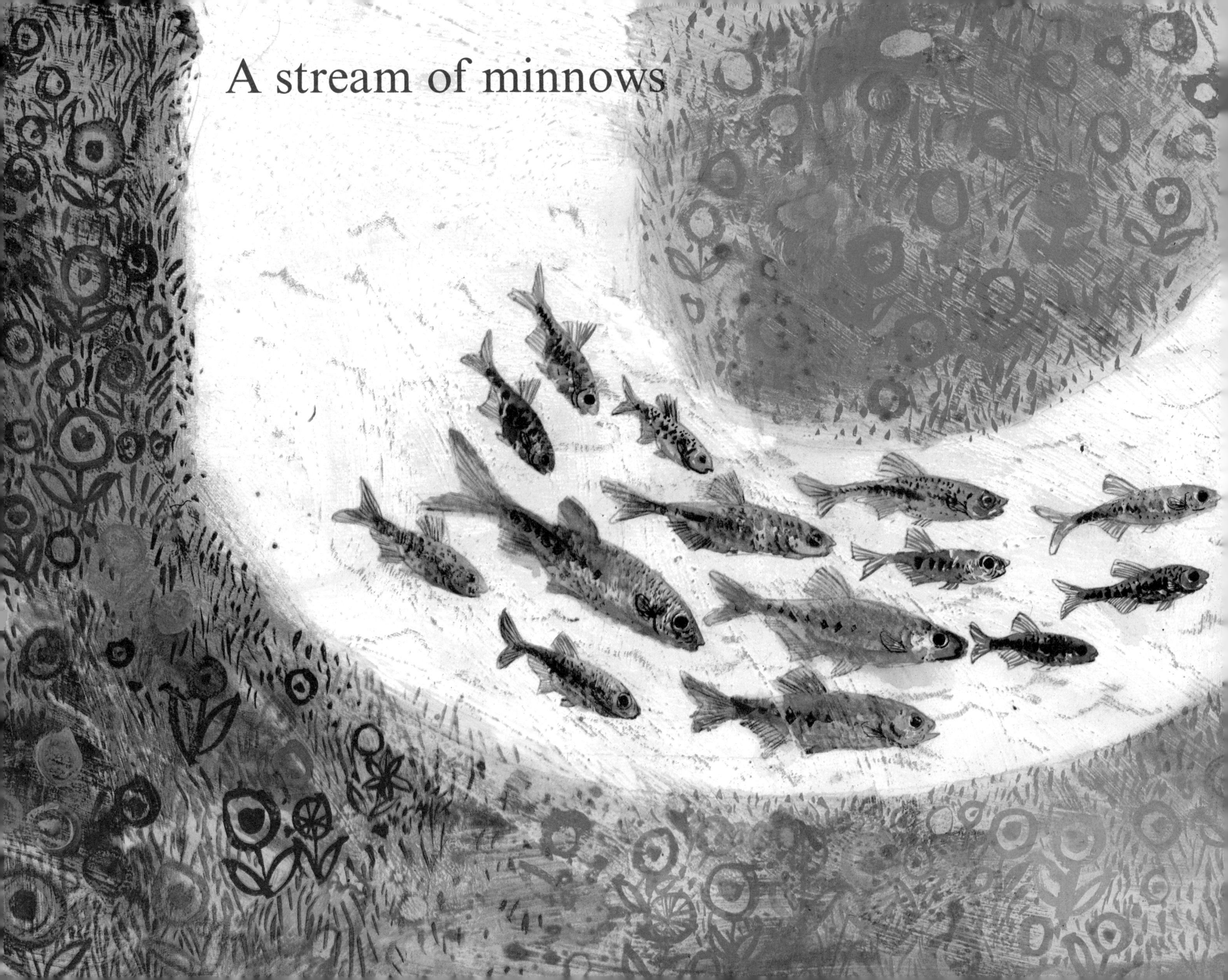

Oxford University Press, Walton Street, Oxford OX2 6DP Oxford
New York Toronto Delhi Bombay Calcutta Madras Karachi Petaling Jaya Singapore
Hong Kong Tokyo Nairobi Dar es Salaam Cape Town Melbourne Auckland
and associated companies in Berlin Ibadan

Oxford is a trade mark of Oxford University Press

Reprinted 1970, 1974, 1984, 1985, 1986, 1989, 1991

ISBN 0 19 272151 8 (paperback) First published 1985
Reprinted 1986, 1989, 1991, 1992

Reprinted by arrangement with Oxford University Press, Inc.
Printed in USA.

10 9 8 7 6 5 4 3 2 1

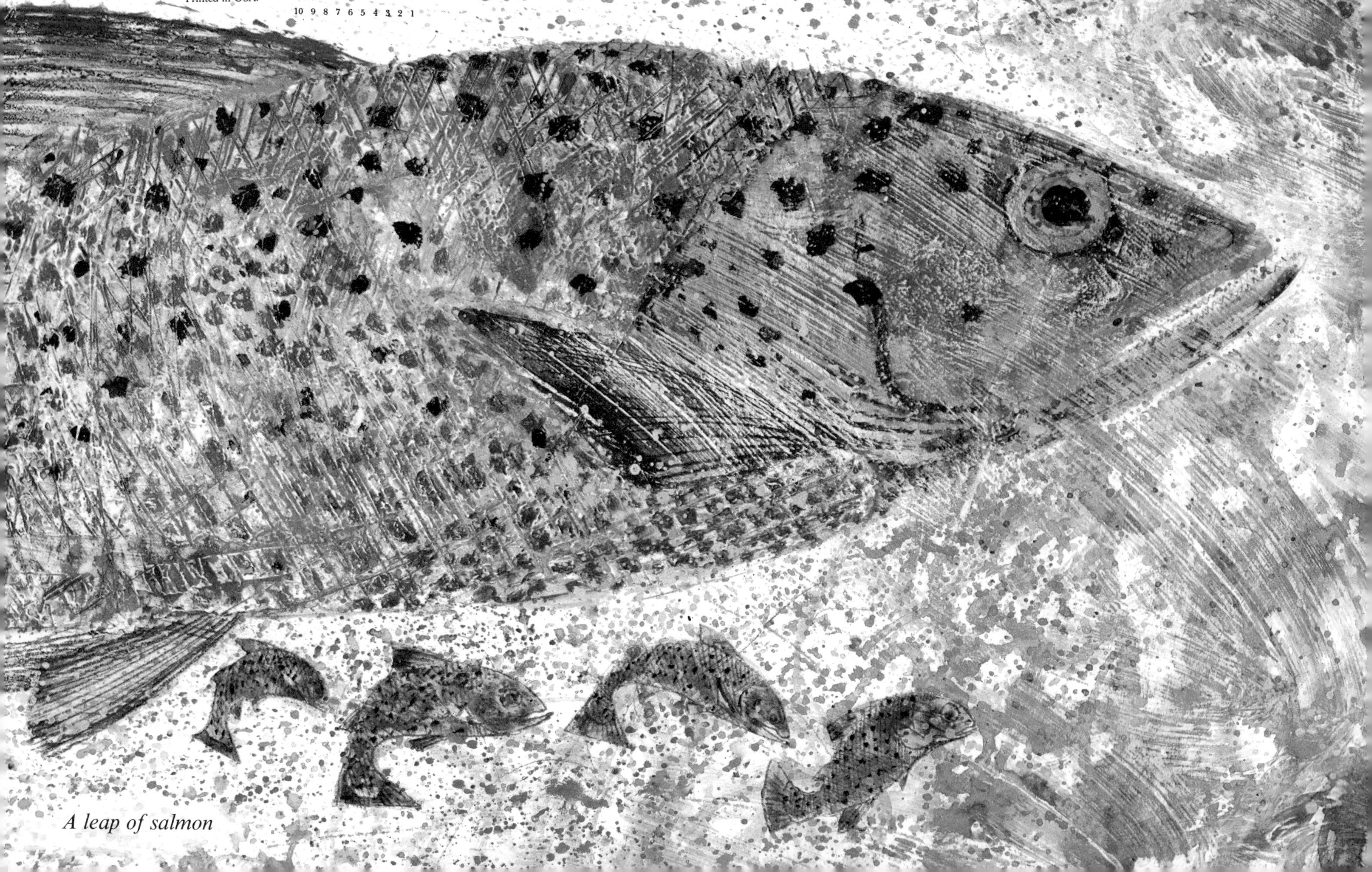

A leap of salmon